DATE DUE

RIMONAH
of the
FLASHING SWORD

A North African Tale

adapted by

ERIC A. KIMMEL

illustrated by

OMAR RAYYAN

Holiday House / New York

AUTHOR'S NOTE

I came upon a traditional version of this story in *Miriam's Tambourine*, Howard Schwartz's collection of Jewish folktales from around the world. According to Schwartz, the story comes from Egypt. The idea of a North African Snow White intrigued me. I was also inspired by a comment of Jane Yolen's, that the heroines in older versions of traditional tales are far more dynamic than the Grimm brothers portray them. Elements of those older tales went into writing this story, as well as contemporary ideas about women's roles.

—*Eric A. Kimmel*

ILLUSTRATOR'S NOTE

Even though the story is Egyptian in origin, its timeless familiarity led me to place it not in Egypt, but in the more ambiguous world of folklore. Hence there are influences of ancient Egypt, Judaea, Persia, the Ottoman Empire, and Morocco.

—*Omar Rayyan*

To Trina and Barbara
E.A.K.

To Sheila and the flashing cats
O.R.

Text copyright © 1995 by Eric A. Kimmel
Illustrations copyright © 1995 by Omar Rayyan
Printed in the United States of America
All rights reserved
First Edition

Library of Congress Cataloging-in-Publication Data
Kimmel, Eric A.
Rimonah of the Flashing Sword : a North African tale / adapted by
Eric A. Kimmel ; illustrated by Omar Rayyan. — 1st ed.
p.   cm.
Summary: A traditional Egyptian version of Snow White.
ISBN 0-8234-1093-5
[1. Fairy tales.   2. Folklore—Egypt.]   I. Rayyan, Omar, ill.
II. Title.
PZ8.K527Ri   1995   93-40091   CIP   AC
398.21—dc20
[E]

nce upon a time, beyond the sea, a queen sat by her palace window. She took a pomegranate from a basket. Sighing to herself, she said, "Would that I had a child with skin as dark as this pomegranate, eyes as bright as pomegranate seeds, and a voice as sweet as pomegranate juice."

Heaven heard her words. The good queen did have a child, a lovely daughter with skin as dark as a pomegranate's peel, eyes as bright as pomegranate seeds, and a voice as sweet as the juice of ripe pomegranates. The queen named her Rimonah, which means "Pomegranate."

Rimonah's parents, the king and queen, raised her with love and affection. She never knew the meaning of sorrow until the day she turned seven years old. On that day her mother died.

"Beloved Rimonah, I will always watch over you," the queen said. She pricked her finger and let three drops of blood fall into a crystal vial. "Wear this vial around your neck. The blood will dry in time. If it ever turns red and liquid, you will know that danger threatens." The queen closed her eyes for the last time.

After the queen died, the king vowed never to marry again. But there was a sorceress in the kingdom, a cunning beauty of boundless ambition, whose spells had caused the queen's death. She now plotted to win the crown for herself. She brought the king an enchanted cake. With one bite, he became bewitched and had no will of his own. He married the sorceress before Rimonah's mother was in her grave. The evil new queen's power spread like a weed, while that of the king withered.

Now, the queen possessed several magic treasures which she kept hidden in a tower room. Her favorite was a porcelain bowl. Whenever the queen filled the bowl with water, a face appeared that answered any question she asked it. One night the queen filled the magic bowl and asked, "Who is the fairest?"

The bowl had always replied, "Thou, O Queen, are the fairest in the land." But this night it gave a different answer. "Thou, O Queen, are fair, 'tis true, but dark-eyed Rimonah is lovelier than you."

Seething with jealousy, the queen ordered her huntsman to take Rimonah to the desert and kill her.